Copyright © 2002 by Nord-Süd Verlag AG, Gossau Zürich, Switzerland
First published in the Netherlands under the title *Basja de beer* by
De Vier Windstreken, Niederlande, an imprint of Nord-Süd Verlag AG,
Gossau Zürich, Switzerland. English translation © 2002 by
North-South Books Inc., New York

First published in the United States, Great Britain, Canada,
Australia, and New Zealand in 2002 by North-South Books,
an imprint of Nord-Süd Verlag AG, Gossau Zürich, Switzerland.

Distributed in the United States by North-South Books Inc., New York.

Library of Congress Cataloging-in-Publication Data is available.
A CIP catalogue record for this book is available from The British Library.
ISBN 0-7358-1624-7 (trade edition) 10 9 8 7 6 5 4 3 2 1
ISBN 0-7358-1625-5 (library edition) 10 9 8 7 6 5 4 3 2 1
Printed in Belgium

For more information about our books, and the authors and artists
who create them, visit our web site: www.northsouth.com

Bailey
the
Bear
Cub

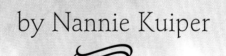

by Nannie Kuiper

illustrated by Jeska Verstegen
translated by J. Alison James

North-South Books
NEW YORK/LONDON

Bailey was a little bear cub. He played all day long. When he was hungry, his mother would pick sweet berries for him. She dug up roots for him to chew. He licked honey from her paws, and she caught him plump juicy fish.

Every night when it grew dark, Mother and Bailey sat by each other and looked at the stars.

"One day you will be a big strong bear," Mother said. "You might even get big enough to reach the stars!"

"When I grow up," Bailey said, "I will be big enough to reach the stars. Then I will get the prettiest star and give it to you."

Bailey grew quickly, and he was always hungry. Mother had to find a lot of food for him.

One day she said, "I can't keep up with you. It is time for you to learn how to find your own food. Come with me."

Bailey scampered after his mother.

"Berries are easy," Mother said. "Lift your nose high in the air and sniff. That is how to find berries."

Bailey lifted his nose high in the air and sniffed. But all he smelled was a squirrel. There it was, running up the tree. Bailey chased after it.

"Well, all right," said Mother. "As long as you're up there, you can look for honey. Just scoop it out of the beehive."

But Bailey was frightened by the terrible buzzing, and he fell off the branch.

"They can't sting you," Mother said. "Your fur is much too thick."

That afternoon, Mother lay down for a nap. But Bailey was too hungry to sleep. He thought he would try to dig for some roots, but the ground was hard, and all he got was dirt in his claws.

Bailey was discouraged. Perhaps he should not grow big and strong after all. If he stayed small, Mother would always bring him food.

"Let's go to the river," said Mother when she woke from her nap. Bailey thought of a juicy fish and his tummy rumbled.

Mother splashed into the river, but Bailey stayed at the edge. "You have to get wet to catch a fish," she said. "Watch how big bears do it."

Bailey decided that he was not big enough to go in that cold water. "The fish might bite me," he said to Mother.

Mother laughed and said, "I think bears' teeth are more dangerous. She swished with her paw and brought out a big fat fish.

Bailey watched her eat. He was so hungry, but catching a fish was too hard for such a small bear.

That night, Bailey looked at the stars. "I'll never be that big," he said to his mother. "I can't even find food for myself. How could I ever get you a star?"

Mother nuzzled him warmly. "Tomorrow you will manage to find food," she promised, and she fell asleep beside him.

But Bailey was too hungry to sleep. Quietly he slipped away from his mother and went into the woods. There was a honey tree. The bees will be sleeping, he thought, and he climbed up quickly. He managed to get a chunk of honeycomb before he tumbled down. He rolled happily in the needles licking his paw.

But he was still hungry.

Bailey found the river and stood at its edge. The water was dark and still. Perhaps the fish were also sleeping, and he could catch one.

Bailey trembled. He put a paw into the water and then he saw them, swimming there—stars! They had fallen from the sky and were floating in the water.

Bailey sprang into the river to catch one to bring back to Mother. But each star he reached for slipped right through his paws. He moved slowly. He skimmed the surface. He moved fast. He reached in deeper.

Suddenly he had something slippery and silver in his paws. It was no star. It was a fish! Bailey took a huge bite.

He heard something. Frightened, he turned around. But it was his mother who stood on the shore, smiling proudly. "Well, I see you have found something to eat," she said.

Mother and Bailey sat beside each other and looked up at the stars. "Stars are hard to catch," Bailey said. "I don't know if I'll ever be big enough to get you a star. What would you say if I caught you a fish instead?"

"I would be delighted," said Mother.

Mother hugged Bailey tight.

"Do you know," she said quietly, "tonight when you caught your first fish, you were so happy and proud that you had stars in your eyes. Those were the loveliest stars to me."

Then Mother Bear and big bear, Bailey, curled up together and went to sleep.